Kwagga Publishers cc
17 Duncan Road, Wynberg 7800
Telephone: (021) 797 2506

© text Dianne Case 1997
© pictures Joanne Harvey 1997

All rights reserved. No part of this publication may be reproduced, stored in a retrieval system, or transmitted in any form or by any means, electronic, mechanical, photocopying, recording, or otherwise, without the prior written permission of the copyright holders.

ISBN 0-620-21978-5

Reproduction by Scan Shop, 15 Wandel Street, Gardens, Cape Town
Printed by Universal Printing, Durban, 72 Stanhope Place, Briardene 4051

The publishers wish to thank Ann Walton for her contribution to this book.

What a Gentleman

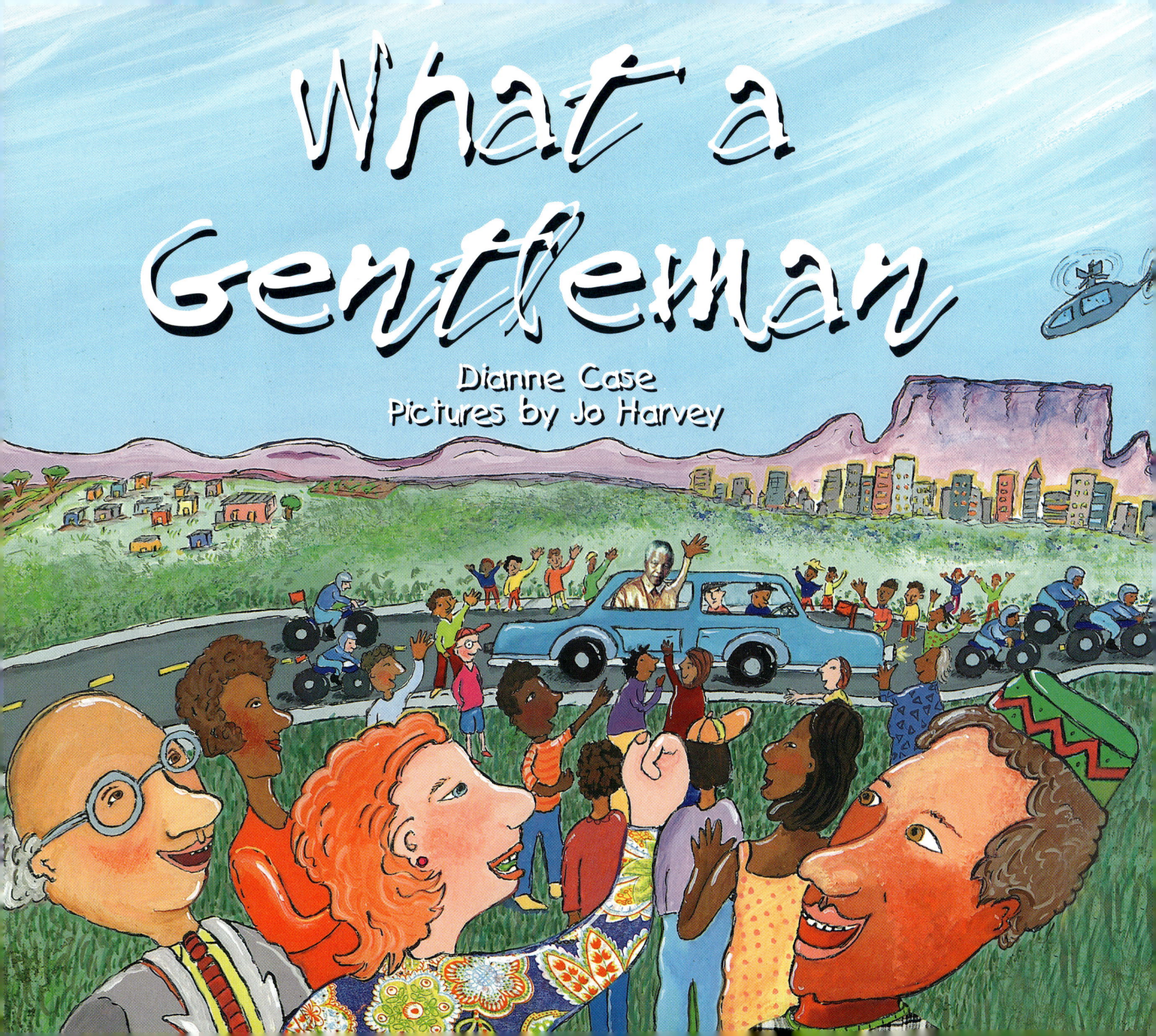

My grandmother loves Mr Mandela. We all know that!

.... and my grandmother knows everything.

My grandmother says Mr Mandela is a very wise man.
'That's why he is the president of our country,' she says.

My grandmother says Mr Mandela cares about ordinary people.
'He goes out of his way to help where he can,' she says.

My grandmother says Mr Mandela believes children are special people.

'That is why children all over South Africa love him so much,' she says.

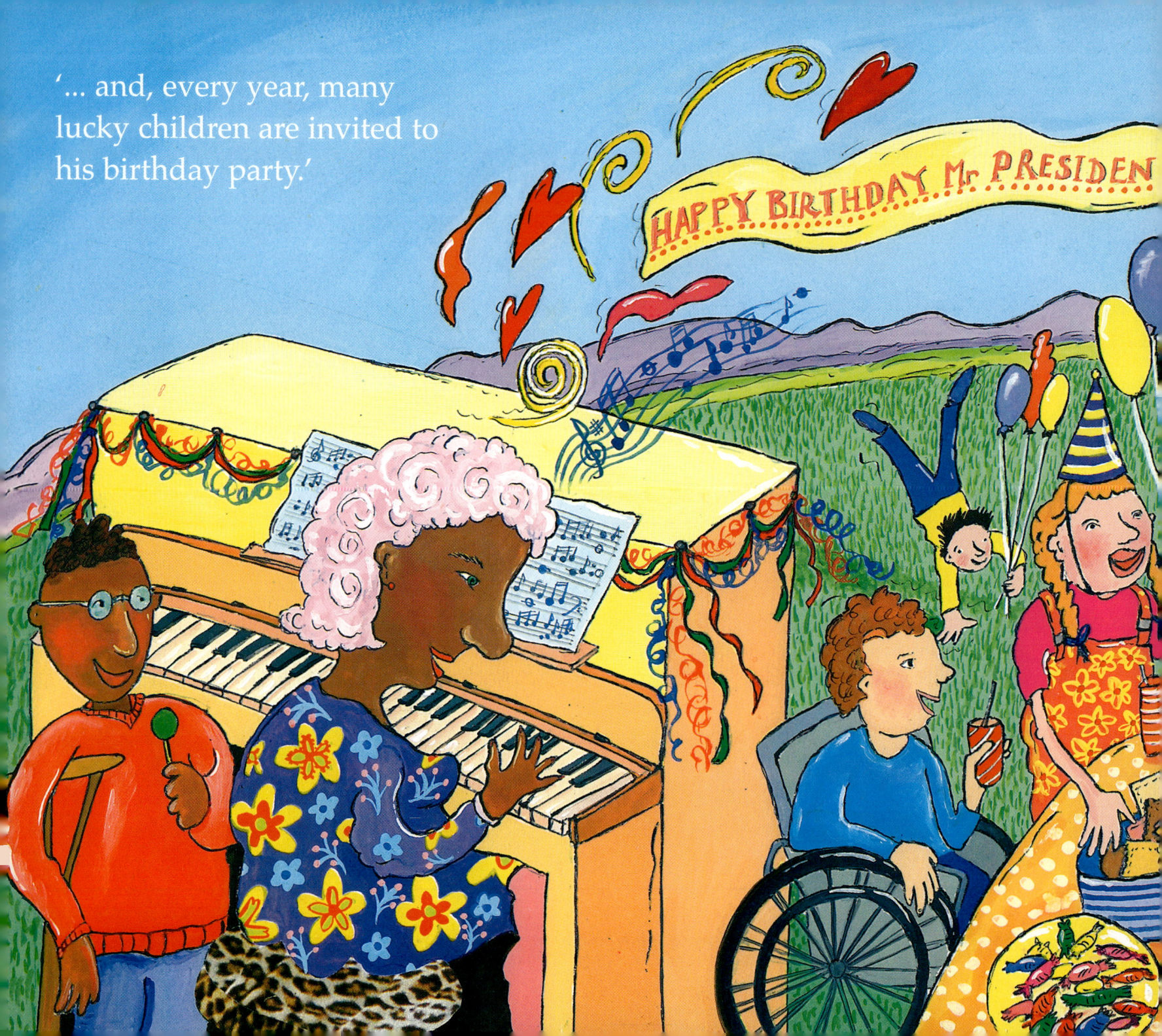

'... and, every year, many lucky children are invited to his birthday party.'

My grandmother says Mr Mandela is an inspiring person. 'He specially wore a Springbok jersey when he watched the final of the Rugby World Cup.'

'That is why we won!' she says.

'And do you know which long-distance runner won a gold medal for our country at the Olympic Games in Atlanta?' she asks.

'Mr Mandela!' my brother answers.
'No! No! No!' my grandmother says. 'Mr Mandela is a statesman, not an athlete!'

'It was Josia Thugwane who won it!' I answer, and burst out laughing, because my brother looks like a silly dog with his tail between his legs.

'And when Mr Thugwane accepted his medal, he said he did it for Mr Mandela,' my grandmother says proudly. 'Can you see how he inspires people?'

My grandmother says
Mr Mandela is kind and gentle.

'That is how people
throughout the world
think of him,' she says.

My grandmother says Mr Mandela gets up early so he can exercise.

'That is why he is so fit and healthy,' she says.

My grandmother says Mr Mandela is a trendsetter.

'He wears the most beautiful shirts,' she says.

My grandmother says Mr Mandela believes families are precious.
'He is a great family man himself,' she says.

My grandmother says Mr Mandela loves nature. 'He planted vegetables when he was on Robben Island, and sometimes gave the warders tomatoes and onions,' she says.

My grandmother says Mr Mandela is handsome and charming.

'He has such a good sense of humour!' she says.

'That is why, wherever he goes, people want to be near him to share in the Madiba Magic.'

'Of course,' I think to myself. 'Given half a chance, my grandmother will be first in the queue!'

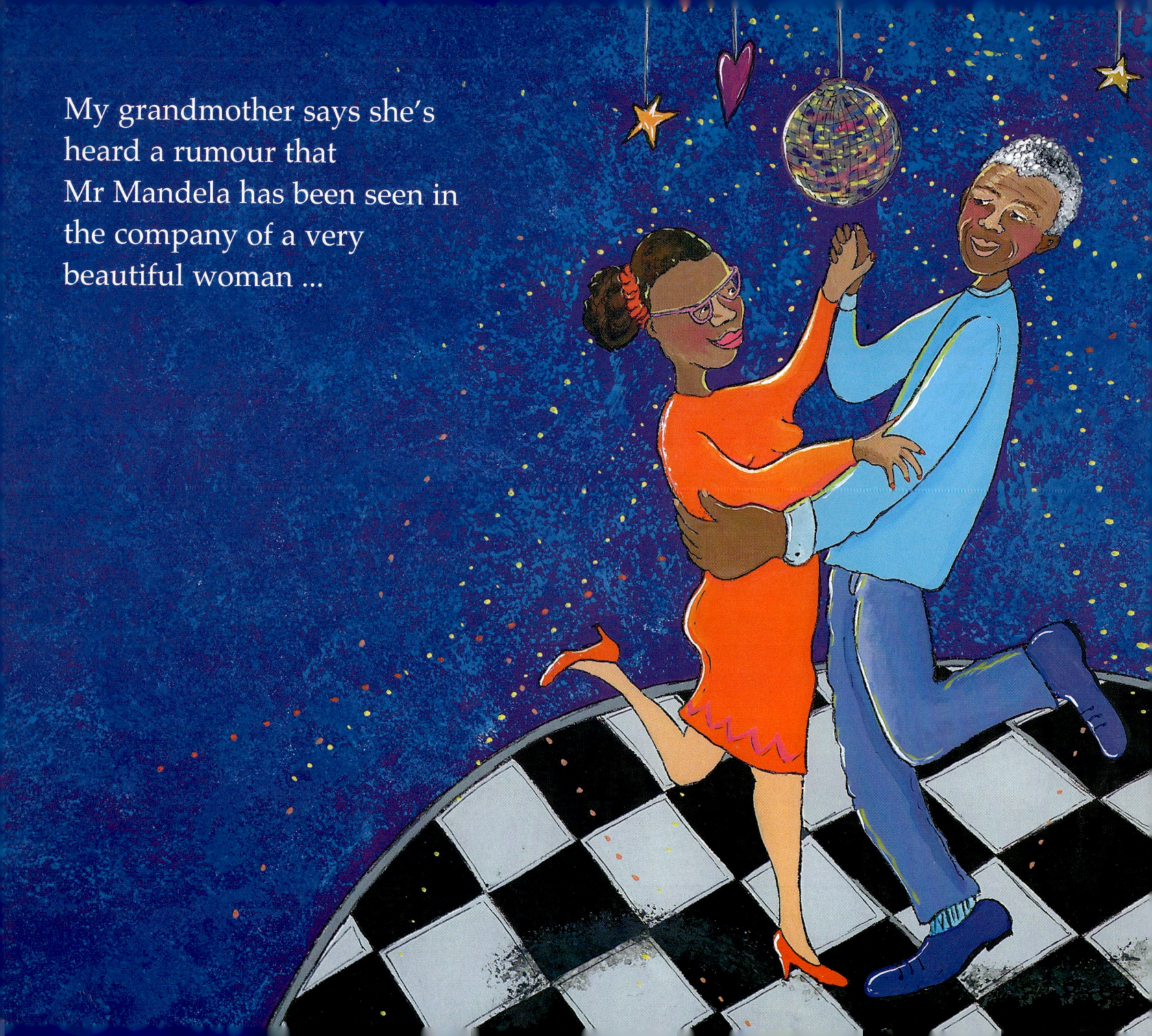

My grandmother says she's heard a rumour that Mr Mandela has been seen in the company of a very beautiful woman ...

'But still,' she says. 'He can put his shoes under my bed anytime ....'